MATT'S IN CHARGE

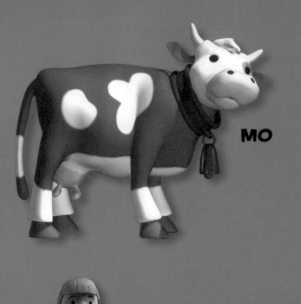

MO

BUZZ

SNICKER

WACK

BACH

FARMER FI

WHEEZY

RORA

DUSTY

THE HENS

PURDEY

REV

RIFF

THE SHEEP

TOM

WINNIE

MATT

First published in Great Britain by HarperCollins Children's Books in 2005

1 3 5 7 9 10 8 6 4 2

ISBN: 0-00-719935-X

Text adapted from the original script by Andrew Brenner

The Contender Entertainment Group
48 Margaret Street, London, W1W 8SE

www.contendergroup.com

Tractor Tom © Contender Ltd 2002

MATT'S IN CHARGE

HarperCollins *Children's Books*

One morning Tom heard a strange sound coming from the yard.

"*Achooo!*"

It was Fi.

"You don't sound very well, Fi," said Tom.

"You're right, Tom. *Achoo!*" sneezed Fi.

"I think I'll call Matt and ask him to look after the farm today."

Just then Fi let out a huge sneeze. The eggs she was carrying went up in the air and all over Tom!

"Yipee!" shouted Matt. "I'm going to be in charge! Come on, Rev let's go!"

At the farmyard Matt asked Tractor Tom and all his friends to line up.

"Hello," he said, proudly. "I'm going to be in charge today, so I am sure we'll get lots of jobs done!"

Tom and his friends weren't so sure Matt would do a good job.

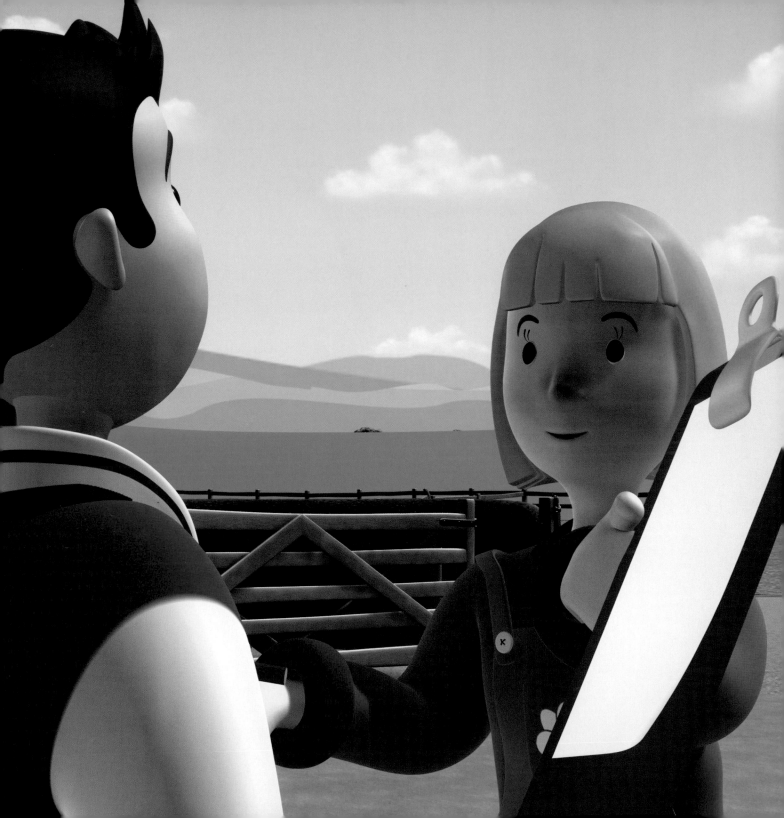

"*Achoo!* Hello, Matt," sniffed Fi, "I have lots of jobs for you to do. Maybe you should write them down?"

Matt said he would remember all the jobs. He didn't need to write them down. Fi wasn't very sure, there were lots of jobs to do.

"I won't let you down," promised Matt. So Fi told him all the jobs.

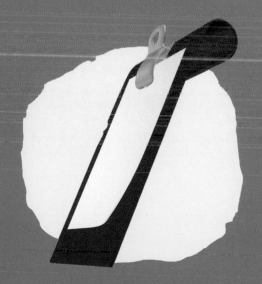

When Fi had gone Tom asked Matt
for his first job.

"Do you remember what the first job was?"
Matt whispered to Rev.

Rev thought it had something to do
with carrot seeds.

"That's right! Plant the carrot seeds."
Matt was so happy he
knew which job to do,
he didn't notice he
had put the chicken
feed in Tom's planter
instead of the carrot seed!

"Tom, tom, tom," said Tom happily, as he went
off to plant the carrot seed. Buzz went with Tom.
He wanted a job too.

When Tom and Buzz got to the field it
hadn't been ploughed.

"Oh, dear," thought Tom.
"We can't sow the
seed until the field
has been ploughed.
Matt forgot to
ask me to plough
the field!"

But Matt had other plans for Tom. Next he wanted Tom to dig holes for the new trees.

"But we don't have the trees yet," Tom reminded Matt.

"Don't worry, Tom. I'll go to town for them right now," said Matt.

Tom was worried that Matt had forgotten other jobs.

"Have you fed the animals yet, Matt?" Tom asked.

"Not yet, Tom," answered Matt.

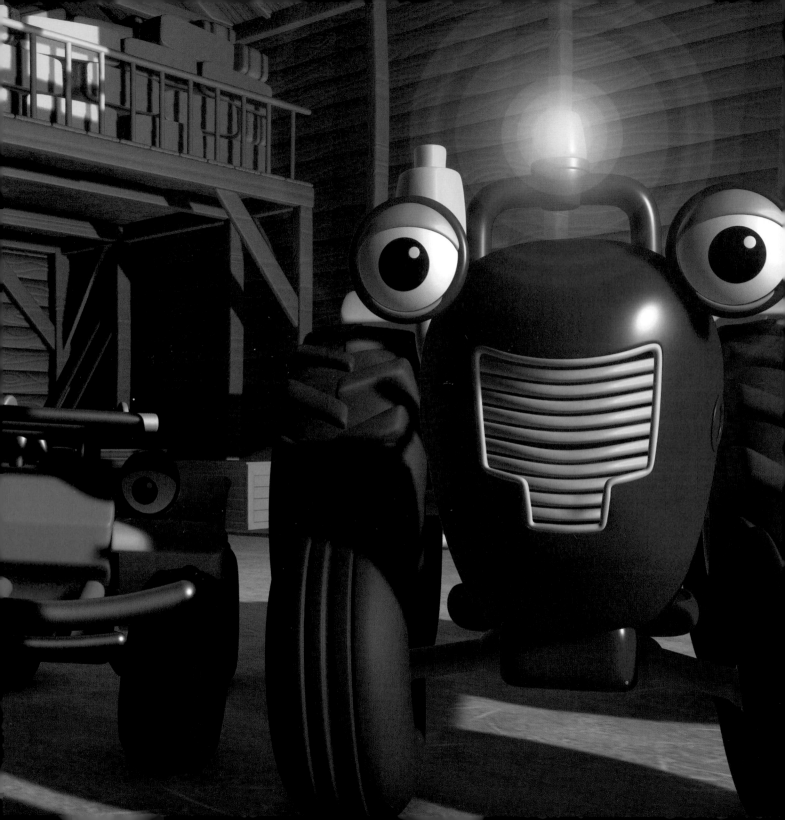

"I'll have to get some more chicken feed when I'm in town. We've run out," added Matt. And he zoomed off in Rev.

Tom went back into the barn.

"Oh, no! Look, Buzz," cried Tom. "Matt has mixed up the chicken feed and the carrot seed. He's put the chicken feed in my seed hopper!"

"Oh, well. I guess we can feed the chickens now."

Tom went to the hen house. It was empty.

He looked for the other animals, but he couldn't find them.

Then Tom heard a very strange noise coming from Fi's kitchen.

"Moo, Neigh, Cluck, Quack!"

The animals were eating Fi's food! Matt had forgotten to feed them.

Fi came to see what all the noise was.

"Don't worry, Fi," said Tom. "Rora, Buzz and I will feed the animals. Go back to bed."

"*Achoo*! Thank you, Tom," said a very tired Fi.

Tom used his seed hopper to feed the chickens. Buzz put hay in Snicker and Winnie's trough. And Rora fed Wack and Bach their corn.

But there were still lots more jobs to do. And Tom didn't want to wake up Fi.

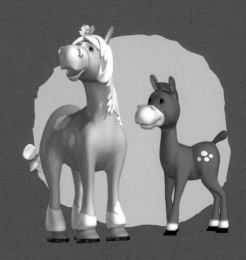

Tom decided *he* would do the jobs.

   He put on his plough and ploughed the field for the carrots.

   Next, he emptied the bag of carrot seed into his planter. He drove to the field and sowed the seeds.

   Then he used his digger to dig holes for the new trees.

Just as Tom was finishing his jobs Matt and Rev came back from town.

Tom and Fi went to meet Matt and Rev.
Rev was carrying the new trees.

"We've been very busy, Tom," said Matt.

"Yes!" smiled Rev. "We've been looking at cool cars in Beckton."

"Shhhh, Rev!" whispered Matt.

"Did you get all the jobs done, Matt?" asked Fi.

"Umm…umm…well…" said Matt, feeling ashamed. He began to tell Fi how he had forgotten to do most of his jobs.

MATT'S IN CHARGE

MATT'S IN CHARGE BUT IT'S TOM TO THE RESCUE!

"No we didn't," smiled Tom. "I ploughed the field, planted the seed, dug the holes and fed the animals. Just like you told me, remember, Matt?"

"Well done, Tom. What would we do without you?" said Fi, happily. "The next time I'm ill you can be in charge."

"*Achoo*!" sneezed Matt.

"And it looks like that might be tomorrow!" laughed Fi.

MO

BUZZ

SNICKER

FARMER FI

WACK

BACH

WHEEZY

RORA

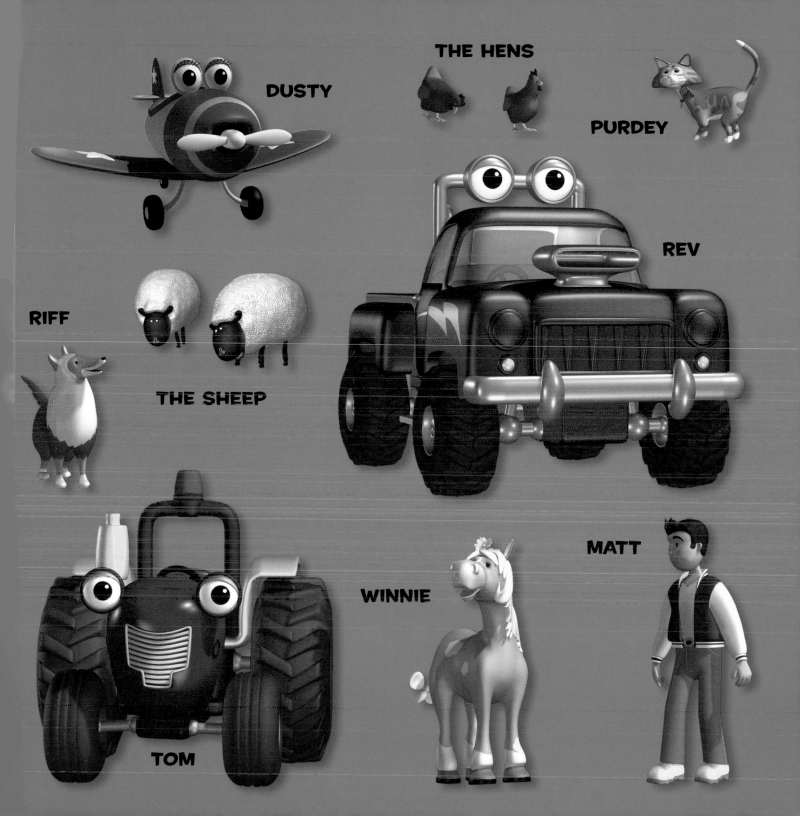

DUSTY

THE HENS

PURDEY

REV

RIFF

THE SHEEP

TOM

WINNIE

MATT

YOU CAN COLLECT THEM ALL!

WHAT WOULD WE DO WITHOUT HIM?